With Love for Amanda and Amy

Text © 1996 by Donald Rubinetti
Illustrations © 1996 by Liisa Chauncy Guida
All rights reserved including the right of reproduction in
whole or in part in any form

Published by Silver Press,
A Division of Simon & Schuster,
299 Jefferson Road, Parsippany, NJ 07054

Designed by Susan Havice

Manufactured in the United States of America
10 9 8 7 6 5 4 3 2 1

Library of Congress Cataloging-in-Publication Data
Rubinetti, Donald.
Cappy the Lonely Camel/by Donald Rubinetti;
illustrated by Liisa Chauncy Guida. p. cm.
Summary: A lonely two-humped camel, taunted and rejected by the
one-humped camels, makes a dangerous journey to save his worst tormentor's sick baby.
[1. Camels—Fiction. 2. Prejudices—Fiction.] I. Guida, Liisa Chauncy, ill. II. Title
PZ7.R831327Cap 1996
[E]—dc20 95-9690 CIP AC
ISBN 0-382-39150-0 (JHC) ISBN 0-382-39151-9 (LSB)
ISBN 0-382-39152-7 (SC)

Cappy the Lonely Camel

by Donald Rubinetti

illustrated by
Liisa Chauncy Guida

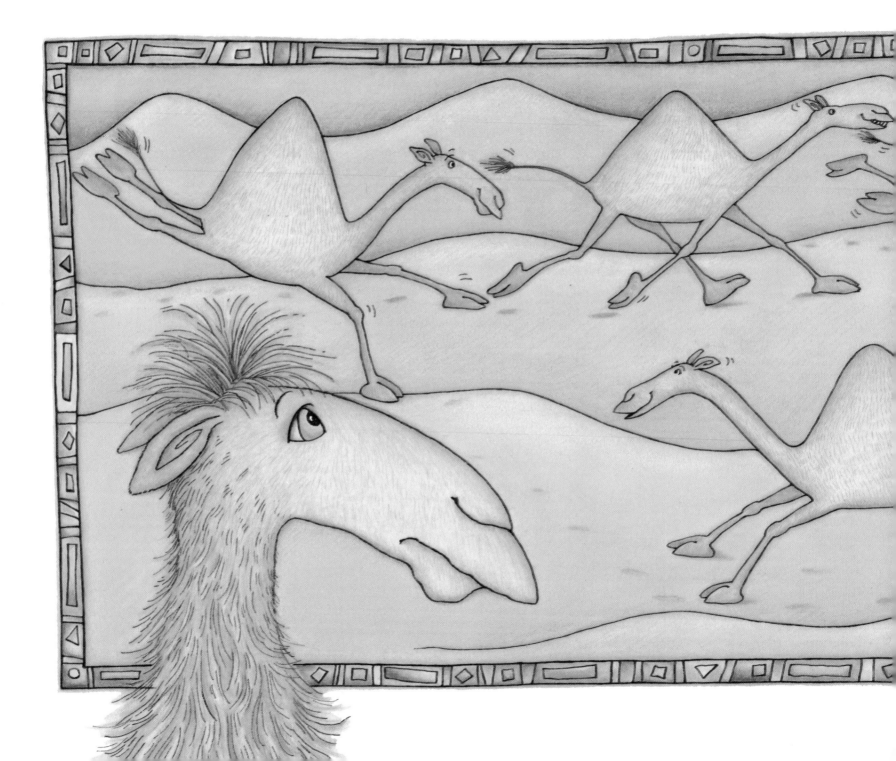

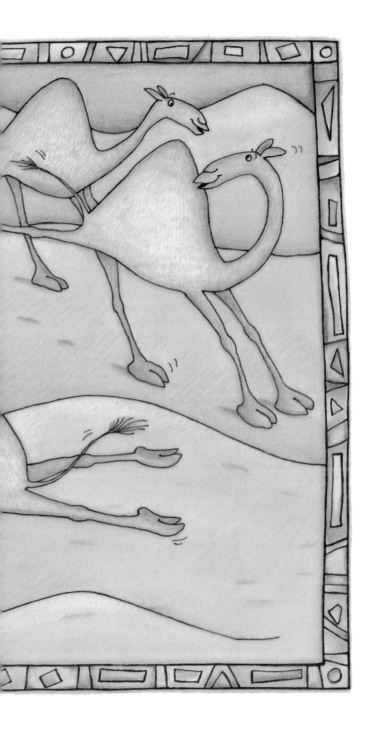

In a little village in Southwest Asia, there lived many young camels. From early in the morning until the evening, they spent time together. Their days were filled with running and games and laughter and great fun. They were very happy young camels . . . all except one.

Cappy was an unhappy and lonely young camel because none of the other camels would play with him. In fact, the other young camels didn't even talk to Cappy, except to make fun of him. You see, he was not like all the other camels in the village. Cappy was shorter and hairier than the others, but the greatest difference was that he had two humps on his back. All the other camels in his village had only one hump.

So when the young camels weren't ignoring Cappy, they were being mean to him, calling him Lumpy, and Hilly, and other names. Cappy's meanest tormentor was Nastella. She nicknamed him Roller Coaster because of the shape of his back, and she made fun of him every time she saw him. Nastella would even spit at Cappy when she was chewing her cud, causing him to jump and twist his body to avoid being hit.

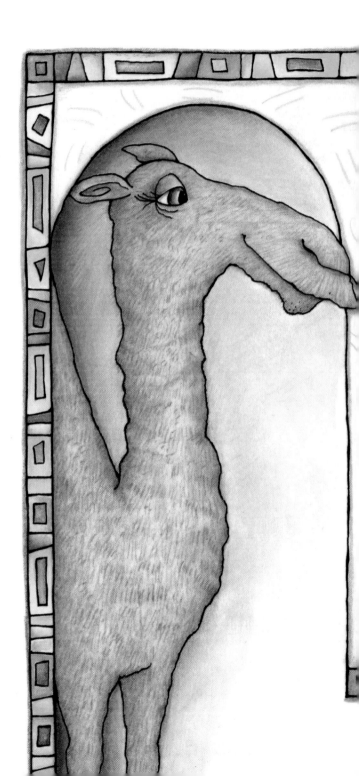

Cappy was an orphan. He had come to this village when he was a baby to live with an elderly friend of his parents. Aunt Materna, as he called his guardian, was now much too old to play with him or even to go outside, so he was really quite alone.

Sometimes, Cappy tried to explain to the other young camels that in Central Asia, far north of their village, there were many camels with two humps. They just laughed at him and shouted, "Roller Coaster! Roller Coaster!" with Nastella leading the chant. After a while, Cappy gave up trying to explain and to be accepted, and he just kept to himself.

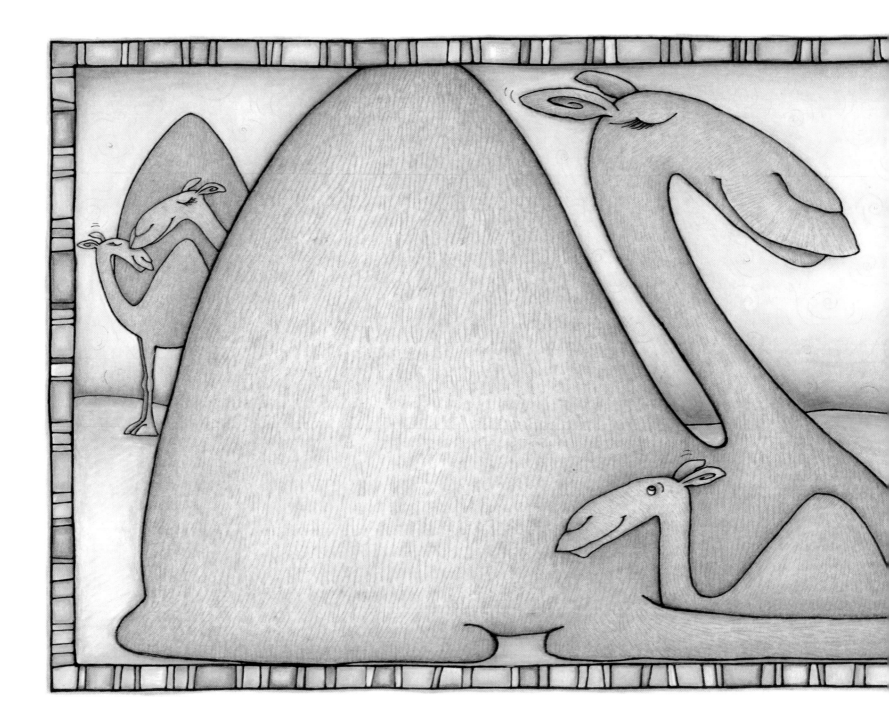

The years passed, and all the young camels in the village grew up and had families of their own . . . all except Cappy. The other camels still spent much of their time together . . . but not Cappy. When they saw Cappy, they still laughed and called him Roller Coaster. Although they didn't play tricks on him anymore, they didn't bother to be friends with him because he was different. To make matters worse, Cappy's aunt had died long ago, leaving him totally alone.

One day, Cappy heard that Nastella's baby was very sick and that the only doctor who could help lived far to the north. That was a terrible problem because they had no way of getting word to the doctor. None of the camels could make the trip because it was wintertime and they couldn't survive the bitterly cold temperatures of the place where the doctor lived. No one could possibly save Nastella's baby . . . no one except Cappy.

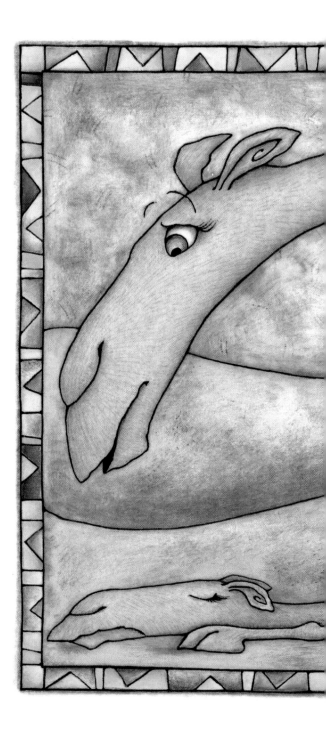

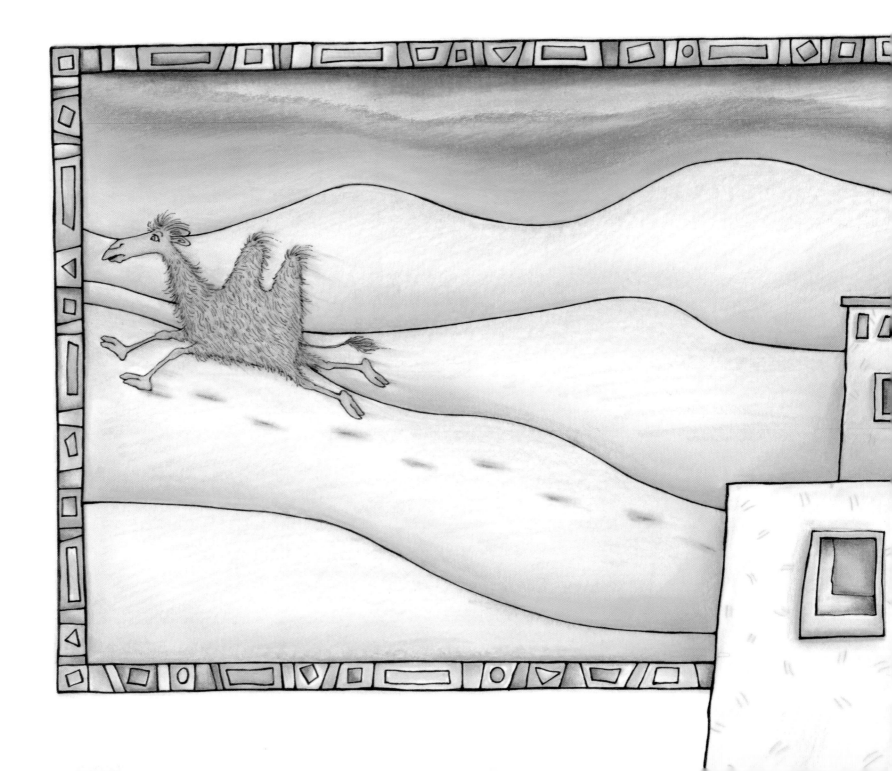

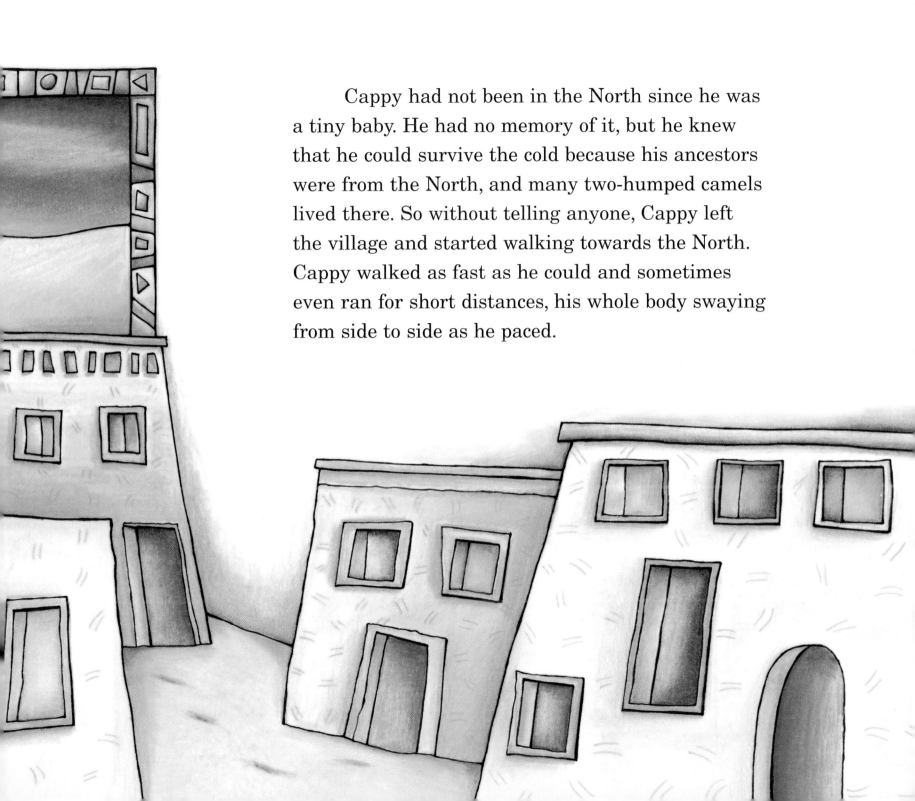

Cappy had not been in the North since he was a tiny baby. He had no memory of it, but he knew that he could survive the cold because his ancestors were from the North, and many two-humped camels lived there. So without telling anyone, Cappy left the village and started walking towards the North. Cappy walked as fast as he could and sometimes even ran for short distances, his whole body swaying from side to side as he paced.

Cappy traveled day and night, stopping only to graze on some grass or bushes or to take a short rest. He walked for many days. The temperature grew colder and colder as he moved northward. The freezing temperatures didn't bother Cappy, but he was very tired and thirsty.

At one point in the journey, Cappy could not find water for four days. His body was so badly shrunken from lack of water that his skin hung loosely like a wrinkled, furry blanket. When he finally came to an oasis, he drank and drank and drank. As he drank, his body regained its natural shape, filling out like an inflatable toy as it's being blown up.

When Cappy reached the town where the doctor lived, he quickly began wending his way along the unfamiliar streets. He hadn't gone far when he spotted the sign on the doctor's front lawn. Upon hearing of the sick baby camel, the doctor immediately climbed onto Cappy's back, settling snugly between his humps as they started the long journey back to Cappy's village.

On the way, they traveled through a terrible windstorm. The doctor shielded her face by hiding in the long hair on Cappy's back. Cappy narrowed his nostrils against the wind and kept his long, thick eyelashes down to protect his eyes from the blowing sand and particles of dirt and twigs.

It was a long, difficult journey, but Cappy and the doctor returned to his village late one night. He left the doctor in front of Nastella's door, and Cappy went home, exhausted.

When she saw the doctor, Nastella was
overjoyed. The doctor felt sure she could make
the baby well. When Nastella asked the doctor
how she knew the baby was sick and how she
got to the village, the doctor replied, "One of
your friends came for me and carried me all
the way to your home on his back. His name
is Cappy."

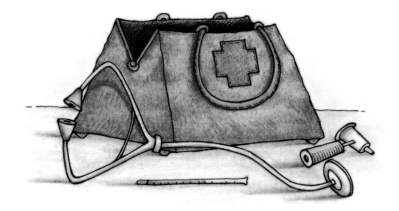

When Nastella heard this, giant tears filled her eyes and splashed down her cheeks. She cried all through the night for all the pain she had caused this brave, gentle camel who had saved her baby.

The next day, Nastella roused the whole village and had them follow her to Cappy's home. When Cappy came out, he was shocked to see all the camels in the village gathered before him.

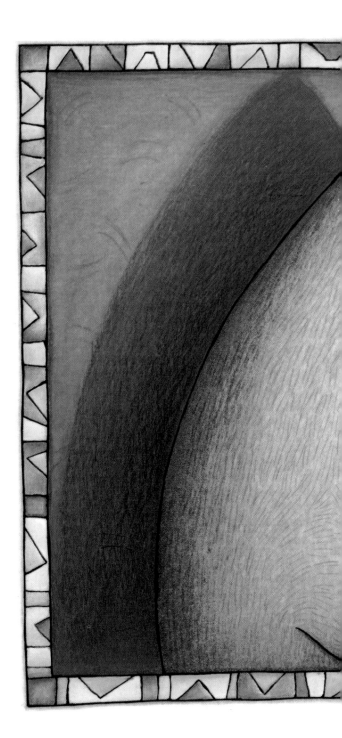

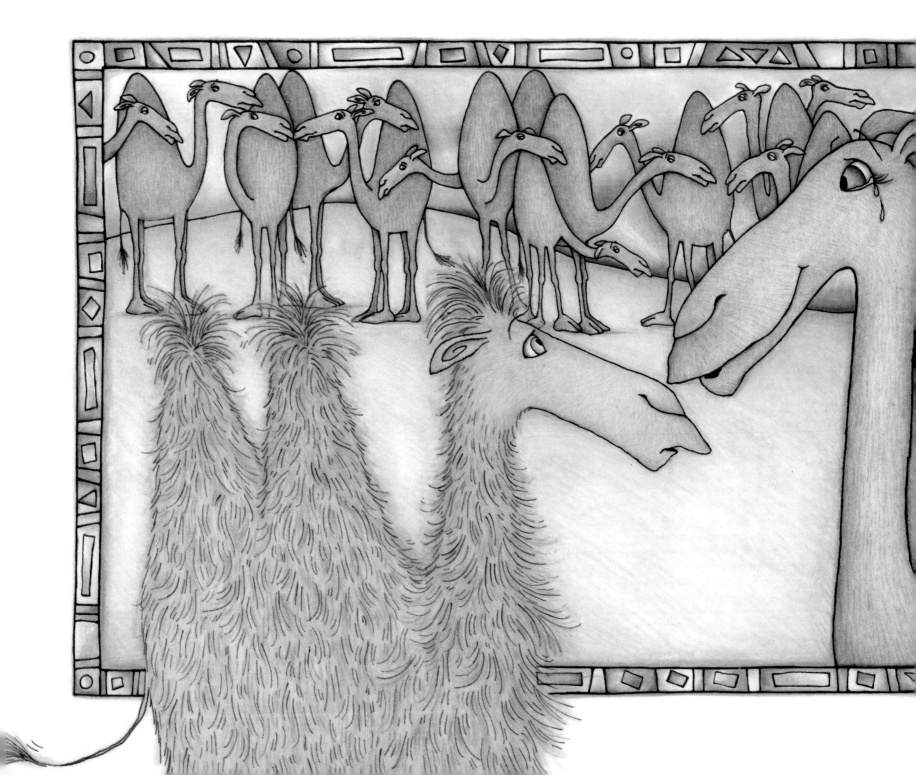

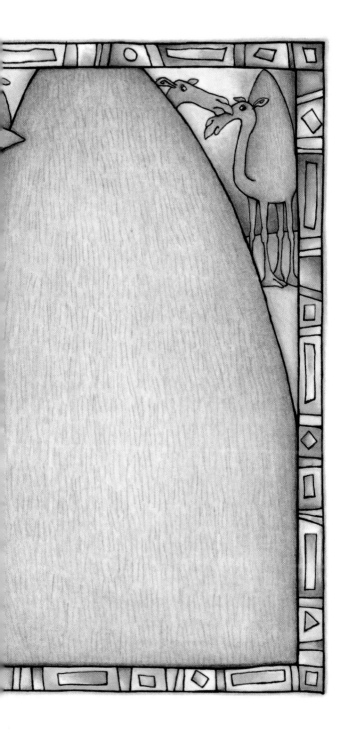

Nastella said, "I have come here for three reasons. The first is to thank you for saving my baby."

"You're welcome," Cappy said with sincerity.

"The second is to ask if you will forgive me for all the unkind things I have done to you."

"And please forgive us, too," shouted the others behind her.

Tears filled Cappy's eyes, and he saw that Nastella's eyes were also moist. "I forgive you, " he said.

"My third reason for coming," Nastella continued, her voice starting to crack and tears now streaming down her face, "is to ask if you will let me be your friend."

"And us," shouted all the camels.

Cappy looked at them and then back at Nastella. "I would like that," he said. He and Nastella smiled at each other through their tears while the entire village cheered. Cappy felt a warmth inside of him that he had never felt before.

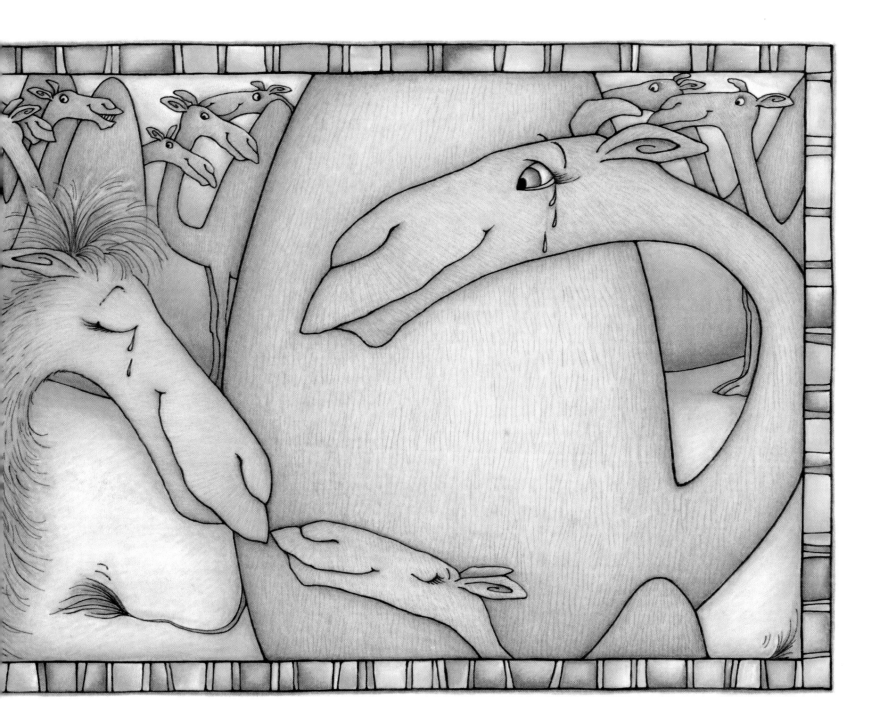

From that day on, Cappy had more friends than he could count. The most devoted of them was Nastella, who named her next baby after him. Now all the camels in the village are happy ... all of them.

About Camels

The one-humped camel is known as an Arabian camel or dromedary. Dromedaries dwell in hot, dry areas such as Northern Africa and Southwest Asia. The two-humped or Bactrian camels can also tolerate hot climates, but they are found principally in Central Asia where the temperature can get quite cold.

Camels are born singly, and as babies, are called foals. A mature dromedary is taller than a Bactrian camel, and is a faster runner. On the other hand, a mature Bactrian camel is more powerfully built and can carry heavier loads.

It is well-known that camels can survive without water for long periods of time. It is, however, a fallacy that they store water in their humps. Camels can withstand a loss of up to one fourth of their body weight from lack of water. Dehydrated camels have been known to drink in excess of twenty-five gallons of water in a very short period of time.